For Madison—

The Twelve Dancing Princesses

Susie Stevenson
1999

The Twelve Dancing Princesses

ADAPTED FROM A STORY BY THE BROTHERS GRIMM

Retold and illustrated by

Suçie Stevenson

A Yearling First Choice Chapter Book

For Richard Morongell

Published by Bantam Doubleday Dell Publishing Group, Inc.
1540 Broadway
New York, New York 10036

Library of Congress Cataloging-in-Publication Data

Stevenson, Suçie.
The twelve dancing princesses / retold and illustrated by Suçie Stevenson.
p. cm.
Originally collected by the Grimm brothers under title: Zertanzten Schuhe.
Summary: An easy-to-read retelling of how the king's twelve daughters wear out their shoes every night while they are supposedly sleeping in their locked bedroom.
Hardcover ISBN 0-385-32167-8 — Paperback ISBN 0-440-41088-6
[1. Fairy tales. 2. Folklore—Germany.] I. Grimm, Jacob, 1785–1863. II. Grimm, Wilhelm, 1786–1859. III. Zertanzten Schuhe. English. IV. Title.
PZ8.S618Tw 1995
398.2′0943—dc20
[E] 94-32512 CIP AC

The text of this book is set in 17-point Baskerville.

Manufactured in the United States of America

October 1995 10 9 8 7 6 5 4 3 2 1

Contents

1. Under a Spell

Once upon a time there was
a lucky dog named Luca.
He was hired to help
the old Royal Gardener
at a splendid palace.

Luca liked his job.
The best part was that each morning
he gave flowers to the Princesses.
There were twelve Princesses.
Each one was beautiful.
"Wowee!" thought Luca.

The Princesses looked like butterflies
in their wide skirts.
They were not very nice, though.
Luca gave them
his most charming smiles.
The Princesses turned up their noses.

"What's with them?" asked Luca.
"Oh, they are under a spell,"
said the old Gardener.
"Their hearts are icy cold."
"No kidding," said Luca.
"It's too bad," said the old Gardener.
"They cannot marry anyone
until the spell is broken."
"How awful!" said Luca.
"It gets worse," said the old Gardener.
"Each night they go out.
They dance until there are holes
in their slippers."
"So?" said Luca.

"No one knows how they escape,"
said the old Gardener.
"Those Princesses are locked up tight
in their bedroom.
There are nine iron doors.
The windows have bars."
The old Gardener shook his head.
"Besides, with twelve Princesses,
that is a lot of slippers."

The King and Queen were fed up.
The Queen tried talking to the Princesses.

"Silk slippers, satin slippers,"
she shrieked,
"slippers, slippers, slippers.
Money doesn't grow on trees, you know!"

The King tried talking to them.
"I COMMAND YOU
TO STOP DANCING!" he bellowed.
"I AM THE KING HERE!
STAY IN YOUR ROOM!"
"There now," said the King to the Queen.

By morning there was another heap
of dancing slippers.
“I can’t bear to look,” said the Queen.
“Ruined,” said the Maidservant.
“Goners,” said the Footman.
“THOSE GIRLS ARE IMPOSSIBLE!”
screeched the Queen.
“More locks! NOW!”
Nothing stopped
the twelve beautiful Princesses.

2. What an Offer!

Finally the King took action.

YOU CAN MARRY THE PRINCESS OF YOUR CHOICE!
Just find out how the Princesses wear holes through their slippers night after night *Positive proof is required*

The King signed the Royal Paper
and sealed it with wax.
"Let's get cracking!" he said.
"I want copies posted
in every town square. Pronto!"
"Calm yourself, dearheart,"
said the Queen.

Dukes and Princes arrived
at the Palace gates from all over.
"What an offer!" said one Prince.
"Out of my way!" said another Prince.
"I was here first," called a Duke.
"Welcome one and all!" said the King.

Every night, a different young fellow guarded the Princesses' bedroom.

Each one vanished by morning.
Dukes and Princes kept disappearing.

Suddenly the other suitors lost interest.
"I'm a gentleman," said one Prince.
"You may take my turn."
"No, I insist, you go ahead," said a Duke.
"Nonsense," said the Prince,
"be my guest."
What were the King
and Queen to do now?

3. Luca in Love

Luca was in love
with the Littlest Princess.
She ignored him.
Luca screwed up his courage.
He put flowers in the Princess's hand.
"I adore you," he whispered.
"Did you say something?"
said the Littlest Princess.
"Um— Um—
Nice dress, is it new?" stammered Luca.

That night, Luca dreamed
about a beautiful Fairy.
"Win your Princess," the Fairy cooed.
"I don't know how," said Luca.
"And why are you flying around
in my dream?" he added.
"Listen up," said the Fairy.

"There is a little bay tree
way in the back of the Royal garden.
Love that tree, Luca.
Hoe it. Water it well.
When it is tall and strong
it will give you wishes."
"Jeepers!" said Luca. "Thanks."

Luca did just as the Fairy said.
The tree sprang up like magic.
When it was green and tall
Luca made his wish.
"Please, dear Tree,
make me invisible whenever I want."

BAPPITY-BAP!

The tree burst into bloom.

Luca picked a flower

and stuck it in his collar.

He turned invisible.

Luca took the crimson flower off.

He could be seen again.

"Yahoo!" said Luca.

4. Gold, Silver, and Jewels

That night the Footman locked the Princesses' bedroom door. Luca, wearing his flower, had slipped inside.

CLANG! CLUNK! CLANK!

Nine iron doors were slammed shut.

Nine keys turned in nine different locks.

HHhhreeeeek! Nine giant bolts

slid into place.

"Peace at last, I hope," said the Queen.

The twelve Princesses jumped
on their beds with excitement.
"I'm wearing only pearls tonight!"
giggled a Princess.
"You'd better wear more than that!"
said another.
Silk petticoats sailed through the air.
Jewelry flew.

The Princesses pulled out
a rainbow of dresses
from the closets.
"These girls are not ready
for bedtime," thought Luca.
He watched as all the Princesses
tried on new satin slippers.

TAP! TAP! TAP!

The Eldest knocked on her bed.

The bed creaked open.

A steep set of stairs appeared.

“YOW!” yelped Luca.

“Who said that?” asked a Princess.

Down the long, dark steps
went the twelve Princesses.
Luca followed.
He stepped on a royal skirt by mistake.
"Hey!" said the Littlest Princess.
She looked back, but no one was there.
Down and down they went.

At the bottom was a path.
Pure silver trees sparkled
in the moonlight.
"Yowee!" thought Luca.
He snapped off a twig
to put in his pocket.
CRACK!
"Hey!" said the Littlest Princess.
"Did you hear that?"
"Hear what?" said the Eldest.

The Princesses walked by trees
with shiny gold leaves.
They walked under trees
glittering with jewels.
Luca grabbed a twig from each.
CRACK! CRACK!
"Everybody stop!" cried the Littlest.
"Listen!"
"Shush!" said the Eldest.
"Or next time *you* are staying home!"

5. No Wonder!

The Princesses came to a lake.
An island rose from the mist.
A magical Palace could be seen.
Music drifted across the water.
Twelve little gold boats
rested on the lakeshore.
Each had an Oarsman ready to row.

The boats glided over the water.
The Littlest's boat fell behind.
"The boat is so heavy tonight!"
said the Oarsman.
Luca, invisible of course,
had jumped into the boat.
He sat right beside the Littlest Princess.
He gave her silky ear a yank.

“Ow!” shouted the Littlest.

“Now what?” called the Eldest.

When the boats reached the island, the Princesses raced up the sand to dance with handsome partners. The partners were the very same Princes and Dukes who had vanished from the King’s Palace.

Luca followed the Littlest Princess
and slipped through the gates.
The huge ballroom was dazzling.
Emeralds, sapphires, and rubies
studded the pearl walls.
Candles glowed.
The music was wild.

Luca couldn't help himself.
He danced from one room to another.
The Princesses whirled by him
in the arms of their suitors.
They danced until their slippers
were in tatters.
"No wonder!" thought Luca.

Just before dawn
the twelve Princesses were rowed
back across the lake.
"See you tomorrow night?"
asked a Prince.
"You bet!" said a Princess.
Each Princess got a good-night kiss
in the moonlight.

The Princesses ran for their bedroom. They wiggled out of their party clothes and fell into bed.

6. Answers at Last

By sunup, the King was furious.
A new pile of torn slippers lay at his feet.
"I DEMAND ANSWERS!"
he thundered.

Later that morning,
Luca gave the Littlest
a special bouquet.
It had a twig of silver, a twig of gold,
and one of diamonds and jewels.
"Did you follow us?" she asked.
"It's not possible!"
"Anything is possible for a clever dog,"
said Luca.
Then he kissed her paw.
"My hero!" sighed the Littlest.
The spell was broken.
"Let's go show the King," said Luca.

"At last!" roared the King. "ANSWERS!"
"You, Luca," said the King,
"may choose any Princess for your bride."
The Littlest batted her eyes.
Luca walked up and down.
"Ummm," he said. "I pick . . ."
"I love you," whispered the Littlest
as he passed by.
"YOU!" said Luca,
and swept her off her feet.

The Queen sighed happily.
The King looked at his other daughters.
They were moony for their Princes
and Dukes from the magical Palace.
"Hhaaarumph."
The King cleared his throat.
"Marriages for everyone!"
declared the King.

A giant wedding was held.

All the Princesses lived happily ever after.

THE END